Will's Boomerang

Stornoway Primary School
Jamieson Drive
Stornoway
Isle of Lewis
HS1 2LF
Tel: 01851 703418/703621
Fax. 01851 706257
E Mail: stornoway-primary@cne-siar.gov.uk

KT-162-049

For my little cousin, Jacob with lots of love – SG

First published 2007
Evans Brothers Limited
2A Portman Mansions
Chiltern Street
London W1U 6NR

Text copyright © Stella Gurney 2007
© in the illustrations Evans Brothers Ltd 2007

All rights reserved. No part of this publication
may be reproduced, stored in a retrieval system
or transmitted in any form, or by any means,
electronic, mechanical, photocopying, recording
or otherwise, without the prior permission of
Evans Brothers Limited.

British Library Cataloguing in Publication Data

Gurney, Stella, 1975-
      Will's boomerang. - (Twisters)
      1. Boomerangs - Pictorial works - Juvenile fiction
      2. Children's stories - Pictorial works
      I. Title
      823.9'2[J]

ISBN-10: 0 237 53336 7 (pb)
ISBN-13: 978 0 237 53336 6 (pb)

ISBN-10: 0 237 53340 5 (hb)
ISBN-13: 978 0 237 53340 3 (hb)

Printed in China

Series Editor: Nick Turpin
Design: Robert Walster
Production: Jenny Mulvanny

TWISTERS

Will's Boomerang

Stella Gurney
and Stefania Colnaghi

Evans

This is Will.

Nice
boomerang!

Boomerangs come back when
you throw them.

Usually.

Better go and find it.

Mind the kangaroos!

Phew!

Keep searching, Will.

Look out!

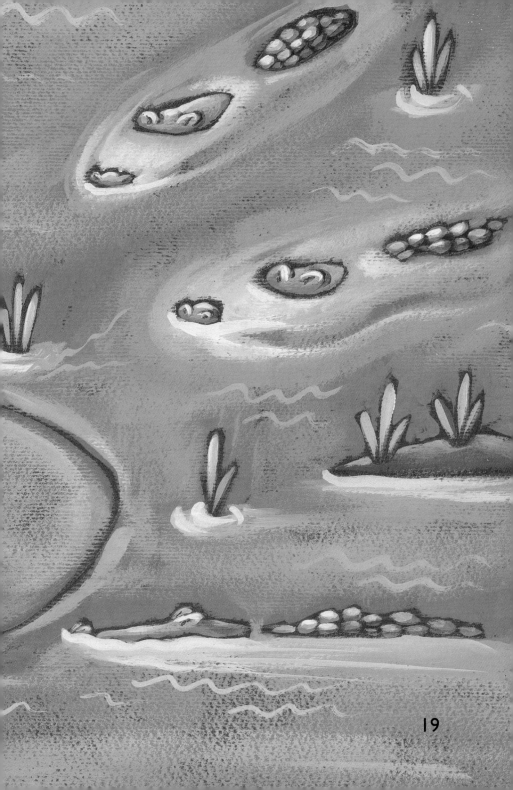

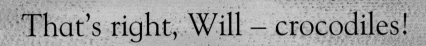

That's right, Will – crocodiles!

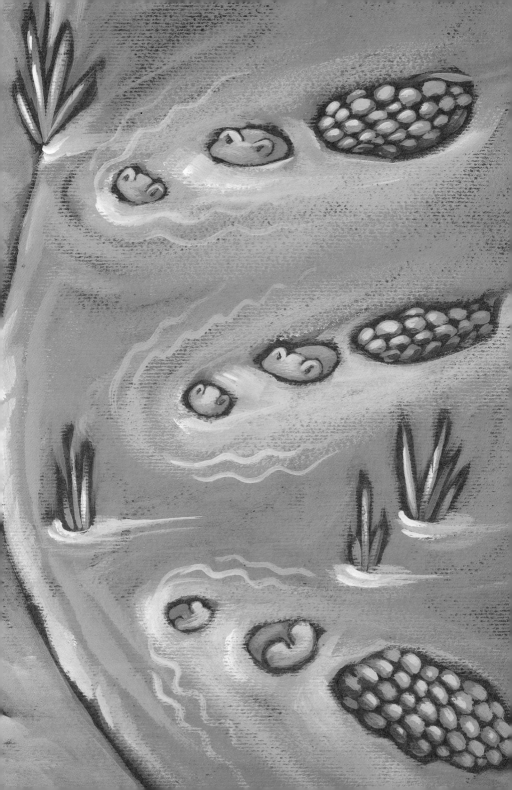

Time to go!

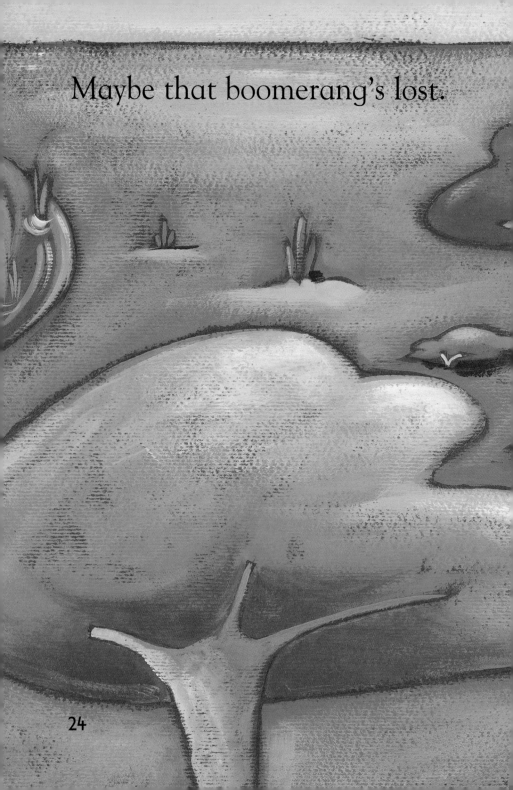

Maybe that boomerang's lost.

A snake!

Will's in trouble now.

Hooray! Will's boomerang came back!

Why not try reading another Twisters book?

Not-so-silly Sausage by Stella Gurney and Liz Million
978 0237 52875 1
Nick's Birthday by Jane Oliver and Silvia Raga
978 0237 52896 6
Out Went Sam by Nick Turpin and Barbara Nascimbeni
978 0237 52894 2
Yummy Scrummy by Paul Harrison and Belinda Worsley
978 0237 52876 8
Squelch! by Kay Woodward and Stefania Colnaghi
978 0237 52895 9
Sally Sails the Seas by Stella Gurney and Belinda Worsely
978 0237 52893 5
Billy on the Ball by Paul Harrison and Silvia Raga
978 0237 52926 0
Countdown by Kay Woodward and Ofra Amit
978 0237 52927 7
One Wet Welly by Gill Matthews and Belinda Worsley
978 0237 52928 4
Sand Dragon by Su Swallow and Silvia Raga
978 0237 52929 1
Cave-baby and the Mammoth by Vivian French and Lisa Williams
978 0237 52931 4
Albert Liked Ladders by Su Swallow and Tim Archbold
978 0237 52930 7
Molly is New by Nick Turpin and Silvia Raga
978 0237 53067 9
A Head Full of Stories by Su Swallow and Tim Archbold
978 0237 53069 3
Elephant Rides Again by Paul Harrison and Liz Million
978 0237 53073 0
Bird Watch by Su Swallow and Simona Dimitri
978 0237 53071 6
Pip Likes Snow by Lynne Rickards and Belinda Worsely
978 0237 53075 4
How to Build a House by Nick Turpin and Barbara Nascimbeni
978 0237 53065 5
Hattie the Dancing Hippo by Jillian Powell and Emma Dodson
978 0237 53335 9
Mary Had a Dinosaur by Eileen Browne and Ruth Rivers
978 0237 53337 3
When I Was a Baby by Madeline Goodey and Amy Brown
978 0237 53334 2
Will's Boomerang by Stella Gurney and Stefania Colnaghi
978 0237 53336 6